Hello, Family Members,

Learning to read is one of the mos nts of early childhood. **Hello Reader!** elp children become skilled readers \ ng readers learn to read by rememb 'ds like "the," "is," and "and"; by using phonics skills to decode new words; and by interpreting picture and text clues. These books provide both the stories children enjoy and the structure they need to read fluently and independently. Here are suggestions for helping your child *before, during,* and *after* reading:

Before

- Look at the cover and pictures and have your child predict what the story is about.
- Read the story to your child.
- Encourage your child to chime in with familiar words and phrases.
- Echo read with your child by reading a line first and having your child read it after you do.

During

- Have your child think about a word he or she does not recognize right away. Provide hints such as "Let's see if we know the sounds" and "Have we read other words like this one?"
- Encourage your child to use phonics skills to sound out new words.
- Provide the word for your child when more assistance is needed so that he or she does not struggle and the experience of reading with you is a positive one.
- Encourage your child to have fun by reading with a lot of expression . . . like an actor!

After

- Have your child keep lists of interesting and favorite words.
- Encourage your child to read the books over and over again. Have him or her read to brothers, sisters, grandparents, and even teddy bears. Repeated readings develop confidence in young readers.
- Talk about the stories. Ask and answer questions. Share ideas about the funniest and most interesting characters and events in the stories.

I do hope that you and your child enjoy this book.

— Francie Alexander
Reading Specialist,
Scholastic's Learning Ventures

To Artie and Cynthia,
proprietors of the Bangall Country Store,
wherein we thought this book up.

Text copyright © 2000 by Daniel Pinkwater.
Illustrations copyright © 2000 by Jill Pinkwater.
All rights reserved. Published by Scholastic Inc.
SCHOLASTIC, HELLO READER, CARTWHEEL BOOKS and associated logos
are trademarks and/or registered trademarks of Scholastic Inc.

Library of Congress Cataloging-in-Publication Data

Pinkwater, Daniel Manus, 1941-
    Big Bob and the Halloween potatoes / by Daniel Pinkwater;
illustrated by Jill Pinkwater.
        p.   cm.— (Hello reader! Level 3)
    "Cartwheel Books."
    Summary: Despite the insistence of her second-grade teacher that their
Halloween celebration will focus on pumpkins, Big Gloria finds a way to introduce
her favorite vegetable, the potato.
    ISBN 0-439-04242-9
    [1. Pumpkin— Fiction.   2. Potatoes— Fiction.   3. Halloween— Fiction.]
I. Pinkwater, Jill, ill.   II. Title.   III. Series.
PZ7.P6335Bek   1999
[E]—dc21
                                                                    98-49687
                                                                    CIP
                                                                    AC

10   9   8   7   6   5   4   3   2   02   03

Printed in the U.S.A.   24
First printing, October 2000

BIG BOB AND THE HALLOWEEN POTATOES

by Daniel Pinkwater
Illustrated by Jill Pinkwater

Hello Reader! — Level 3

SCHOLASTIC INC.
New York Toronto London Auckland Sydney
Mexico City New Delhi Hong Kong

Mr. Salami
Stands His Ground

Mr. Salami is our second-grade teacher. He used to be a cowboy in Montana. He still wears the hat sometimes.

"Class, Halloween is coming," Mr. Salami said.

"Aha!" Big Gloria said.

Big Gloria is the biggest kid in second grade. I am the next biggest after her. I am Big Bob. Gloria is my friend.

"There is no 'Aha!,' Miss Gloria," Mr. Salami said. "Halloween is coming and we will cut out pumpkins to decorate the room."

"Aha!" Big Gloria said.

"You wish to say something?" Mr. Salami asked Big Gloria.

"I wish to say that we should not cut out pumpkins," Big Gloria said. "I wish to say that we should cut out potatoes."

"Sorry," Mr. Salami said. "Not this time. We are doing pumpkins, so get used to it."

Big Gloria raised her hand. "Mr. Salami. Pumpkins mean nothing to us. We do not relate to pumpkins. The only time we ever see pumpkins is Halloween. But... potatoes... we have a great love and respect for potatoes."

"Pumpkins are traditional," Mr. Salami said.

"Potatoes are radical," Big Gloria said.

"I have orange construction paper. I have orange poster paint. I have orange crayons. We will cut out pumpkins," said Mr. Salami.

"Aha!" Big Gloria said.

"Oho!" said Mr. Salami.

"Pumpkins?" Big Gloria asked.

"Pumpkins," Mr. Salami said.

"Not potatoes?"

"I am standing my ground."

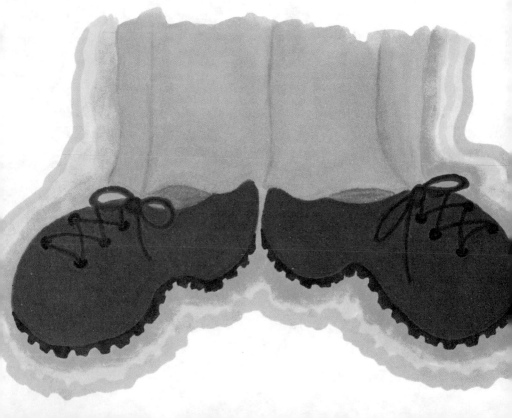

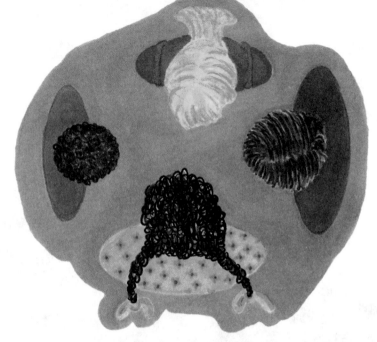

Gloria Grumbles

"Mr. Salami stood his ground," Billy Thimble said. Billy Thimble is a boy in second grade.

"I know," Big Gloria said.

"Most times, you get him to do what you want," Tina Tiny said. Tina Tiny is a girl in the second grade.

"Most times," Big Gloria said.

"He stuck to his pumpkins this time," I said.

"We will see about that," Big Gloria said. "There is more than one way to peel a potato."

Mr. Salami Gets
One Last Chance

The next day, Big Gloria said to Mr. Salami, "You do know that pumpkins are meaningless."

"I deny that," Mr. Salami said. "Pumpkins are useful vegetables. Also, they are pretty. Also, they are orange. The pumpkin is our friend."

"And you refuse to let us decorate with potatoes?" Big Gloria asked.

"I refuse completely," Mr. Salami said.

"You know this is dictatorship," Big Gloria said.

"Yes. I know that," Mr. Salami said.

"Very well," Big Gloria said. Then she was quiet. Then she asked, "Will there be a Halloween party for the second grade?"

"Yes, there will be a party. I am planning it myself," Mr. Salami said.

"And," Big Gloria continued, "will we be allowed to come to the party in costumes?"

"Of course," said Mr. Salami.

"Costumes of our own choice?"

"Certainly," Mr. Salami said.

"Thank you, Mr. Salami," Big Gloria said.

"Will you make pumpkin decorations?" Mr. Salami asked Big Gloria.

"I will," said Big Gloria.

"You are a cooperative girl," Mr. Salami said.

"Dictator," Big Gloria said.

PUMPKIN   JACK-O-LANTERN

PIE

Gloria Has A Plan

"Mr. Salami won," I said.

"Maybe not," Big Gloria said.

"He has decreed a potato-less Halloween," I said.

"Maybe, and maybe not," Big Gloria said.

"Do you have a plan?"

Gloria just smiled.

Gloria's Plan

"Come to my house," Big Gloria told Tina Tiny, Billy Thimble, and me.

"Is this about your plan?" I asked.

"Yes," Big Gloria said.

When we got to Gloria's house, her mother served up potato puffs and glasses of milk.

"This is my plan," Big Gloria said. "For some reason, Mr. Salami has become anti-potato."

"He just insisted we cut out pumpkins to decorate for Halloween," Tina Tiny said.

"Yes! He is pro-pumpkin!" Big Gloria said. "But our Halloween celebration will have potatoes!"

"Have potatoes? How?" we asked.

"We will be potatoes!" Big Gloria said.

"We will?"

"Yes."

"We will? We will be potatoes?"

"Our costumes!" Big Gloria said. "We will go to the Halloween party as potatoes!"

"What a great idea! We can go as potatoes!" Billy Thimble said.

"Of course!" Tina Tiny said. "We can go as anything we like."

"We can tell other kids to go as potatoes," I said.

"Mr. Salami thought there would be no potatoes at Halloween," Big Gloria said. "He thought it would just be pumpkins. Ha."

"Ha," we all said.

Potato People

The day of the party, we met at Big Gloria's house. We would all walk to school together in our costumes.

Big Gloria was dressed as a baked potato. She was wrapped in foil.

I was a french fry.

Billy Thimble was a whole box of french fries.

"My costume hurts," Billy Thimble said.

Tina Tiny was a mound of mashed potatoes.

"Cool costume, Tina," I said.

"We all have cool costumes," Big Gloria said.

We all walked to school together. We were cool potatoes on our way to a party.

The Party Is in the Lunchroom

There was a sign on the door of the classroom.

We went to the lunchroom.

Other second graders were going there, too.
Some of them were dressed as potatoes.

Big Gloria has a lot of influence.

When we got to the lunchroom, there was Mr. Salami. He was wearing a giant pumpkin head.

It was cool.

"What wonderful costumes!" Mr. Salami said. "Welcome to our Halloween party! We will play games! We will dance and sing! We will choose the best costumes! Then we will have good things to eat."

It was a good party. We played games.
We played Pin the Pumpkin on the
Pumpkin. We played Pumpkin, Pumpkin,
Who's Got the Pumpkin? We played
Pumpkin Tag. We played Spin the
Pumpkin.

We also sang songs. We sang Three
Blind Pumpkins, My Pumpkin Lies Over
the Ocean, and Yankee Pumpkin Went To
Town, Riding on a Pumpkin.

We voted for the best costume. It was
Tina Tiny as a mound of mashed potatoes.

Then it was time to eat. Mr. Salami had done all the cooking in the school kitchen.

We had pumpkin soup.

We had roasted, salted pumpkin seeds.

We had pumpkin bread.

We had baked pumpkin slices.

We had pumpkin pie.

We had pumpkin cookies.

It was the best party we ever had.

Gloria Shakes Hands

At the end of the party, Big Gloria went up to Mr. Salami. She was wearing her baked potato costume.

"Mr. Salami, this was the best party we ever had," Big Gloria said.

"Thank you," Mr. Salami said.

"I still think the potato is the King of Vegetables," Big Gloria said.

"It is your right to do so," Mr. Salami said.

"But I do agree that the pumpkin is our friend," Big Gloria said.

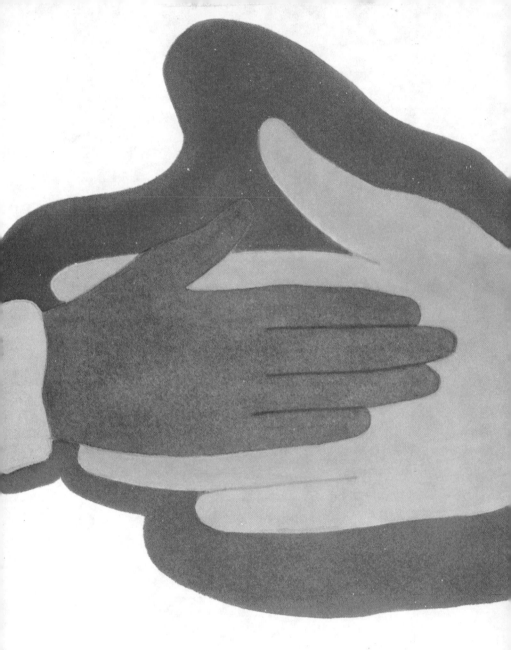

Then Big Gloria and Mr. Salami
shook hands.